White Fang

Treasury of Illustrated Classics

White Fang

by
Jack London

Adapted by
Kathleen Rizzi

Illustrated by
Pete Roberts

Modern Publishing
A Division of Unisystems, Inc.
New York, New York 10022

Series UPC: 39305

Cover art by Pete Roberts

Contents

CHAPTER 1

Danger in the Wild

Spruce trees shivered in a lonely passage of the wild Northland. Down a frozen waterway, a string of dogs toiled tirelessly. Frost coated their bristly fur.

The six dogs were bound with a leather harness. Leather strings attached them to the birch bark sled they worked to pull. The sled did not have runners. It rested on the snow. Many things were attached to the sled. The most prominent was a casket.

Two men toiled with the dogs and kept the sled moving. Both wore wide snowshoes. One struggled as he ran ahead of the sled and dogs. The other struggled as he ran behind. On the sled, in the box, lay a third man, whose struggles were over. The Wild had conquered and beaten him down. Now he was silent, like the opponent that had won the battle.

The wilderness dislikes movement. It freezes water. It drives sap from trees until they are frozen to their mighty hearts. It stops men in their tracks. Yet these two men, covered with frost, kept moving like ghostly specters.

The day had almost ended. When they stopped to set up camp, the two men heard a faint cry of wolves from far away on the still air. Then it slowly died away.

"They're after us, Bill," said the man at the front of the sled.

"No wonder. Meat is scarce," his comrade answered.

Their wolf dogs, gathered on the far side of the fire, snarled and bickered among themselves, but the men knew that the animals would not stray into the darkness.

"Seems to me, Henry, they're stayin'

pretty close to camp," Bill said.

"They know where their hides is safe," Henry said. "They'd sooner eat grub than be grub."

While Bill fed the dogs, suddenly one of the dogs ran across the snow carrying a fish in its mouth. Yet there were still six dogs in camp.

"Did you see that?" Bill asked.

"Yeah," said Henry. "You thinkin' it was one of them?" he added as a wailing cry came from the darkness.

Bill nodded as cry after cry, and answering cries, broke the silence. The dogs betrayed their fear by huddling together. They were so close to the fire that the heat scorched their fur. Bill threw more wood into the fire.

"Henry, this man's luckier than we'll ever be," Bill said, nodding toward the casket. "When we die, we'll be lucky if we get enough stones over our carcasses to keep the dogs off of us. We can't afford a proper funeral. This man was a lord or something in his own country."

"Poor chap. He might have lived to a ripe old age if he'd had the sense to stay at home," Henry agreed.

Bill didn't speak. Instead, he pointed toward a pair of eyes that gleamed like live coals in the darkness. Then Henry saw a second pair of eyes, and a third. A circle of gleaming eyes had drawn around their camp.

Their dogs became uneasy and scrambled around the men and the fire.

"Henry, too bad we don't have more ammo," Bill said. "I wish we had never started on this trip and that we were already at Fort McGurry."

Henry grunted in agreement.

The men slept, breathing heavily, as the fire died down. The gleaming eyes drew closer to the camp. Their dogs drew together in fear, closer to the fire that protected them.

The next morning, Henry awoke first. It was six o'clock, but it was still dark. He prepared breakfast, while Bill rolled the blankets and prepared the sled for their travel.

"Fatty is gone," Bill said.

Henry stopped cooking and counted the dogs. "Five of 'em," he said. "They must have gotten to Fatty in the night. They swallowed 'im alive. I bet he was yelpin' as he went down their throats!"

"Always was a fool dog," Bill said.

"But no fool dog ought to be fool enough to go off that way," Henry said.

He looked over the rest of the team. "I bet none of the others would do it."

"No, you couldn't drive 'em away from the fire with a club," Bill agreed.

"I always did think there was somethin' wrong with Fatty," Henry added.

CHAPTER 2

The She-Wolf

After breakfast, the men started traveling again. The wolves' cries began soon afterward.

Daylight came at nine o'clock. They traveled until three o'clock, when the sun faded and the sky to the south warmed to rose color. The Arctic night fell upon the silent land.

The hunting cries on every side drew closer to them. This scared the sled dogs, causing them to fall out of their traces and upset the sled. Finally, Bill and Henry decided to stop.

Bill went off to look around, while Henry began to set up camp. Then, Henry was startled by a shout from Bill.

When he returned, Bill was holding half of a salmon.

"Must be a tame wolf comin' in here at feedin' time! It got half of what it wanted," he announced, "but I got a whack at it jes' the same. D'ye hear it squeal?"

After a silent dinner, Bill and Henry sat around the campfire. "I wish they'd find a bunch of moose or something, an' go away an' leave us alone," Bill said uneasily.

In the morning, Bill shook his head and said, "Frog's gone."

Henry leaped out from under the blankets and ran to the dogs. He counted them carefully. They had been robbed of another dog.

"Frog was the strongest dog of the bunch," Bill said.

"An' he was no fool dog, neither," Henry added.

They harnessed the four remaining dogs to the sled. The day followed the same pattern as the days before. The

men were pursued by the wolves, whose constant cries panicked their dogs.

That night, after the men tied up the dogs, glowing pairs of eyes appeared out of the darkness that surrounded them. Once in a while, they saw the shadows of the animals that lingered there.

A dog called One Ear was uttering quick, eager whines, lunging at the length of his stick toward the darkness.

"Bill," Henry whispered, pointing out a doglike animal that approached their camp. "Take a look at that."

"It's a she-wolf," Henry said. "That accounts for Fatty an' Frog. She's the decoy for the pack. She draws out the dogs an' then the rest pitch in an' eats 'em up. She's probably been among sled dogs before. That's why she's wise to feedin' time."

"We can't afford to lose no more dogs," Bill said. "If I get a chance, I'll shoot her."

"Remember you've only got three cartridges," Henry objected.

"I'll wait for a dead-sure shot," Bill answered.

In the morning, Henry woke up to find another dog missing. "Spanker's gone," he said. "One of the other dogs must have chewed him loose."

"Well, Spanker's troubles is over, anyway," Bill said.

Hours later into this gloomy day, Bill took the rifle from under the sled lashings, while Henry continued on the trail.

Bill wanted to see the wolves. After an hour, Bill caught up to Henry.

"I seen some of them. They're pretty thin. They must be starving and nearly desperate. They're followin' us and lookin' for game at the same time," Bill said, shaking his head.

A few minutes later, they noticed the she-wolf. It was following their trail.

Bill stopped the dogs. The men watched the strange animal that had led half of their dog-team to their deaths. It was large for a wolf.

"Looks for all the world like a big, husky sled-dog," Bill said. "I wouldn't be surprised to see it wag its tail."

The she-wolf remained alert and regarded them hungrily. They were meat, and the she-wolf was starving. When Bill took the rifle from the sled, the she-wolf leaped sidewise into a clump of spruce trees and disappeared. The two men looked at each other in surprise.

Bill shook his head. "Of course, a wolf that knows to come in with the dogs at feedin' time knows about guns. I'm goin' to get her, Henry. She's too smart to be shot in the open. I'll bush-whack her as sure as my name is Bill."

They set up camp early that night. Three dogs could not drag the sled as fast or for as long as six could. During the night, they fed the fire from time to time to keep the wolves away.

"They're goin' to get us," Bill said. "They're sure goin' to get us, Henry."

"A man's half-licked when he says he is," Henry said. "An' you're half-eaten from the way you're goin' on about it."

CHAPTER 3
Rescued

When the morning came, the men were relieved to see that they had not lost any dogs during the night. At midday, the dogs overturned the sled on a rough piece of trail. Bill and Henry tried to straighten it out, as One Ear walked away.

They called to him, but he didn't listen. The she-wolf waited for him. One Ear was alert and cautious. He tried to touch his nose to hers, but she retreated playfully. Step by step, she lured him away from the security of his human masters.

Bill raised his rifle, but One Ear and the she-wolf were too close together. He

could not risk a shot. When One Ear realized his mistake, he turned and started to run back toward the men, but a dozen wolves came out of the woods and began to cut him off. Bill took his rifle and went after One Ear.

"Bill!" Henry called after him. "Be careful! Don't take no chances!"

Henry sat down on the sled. Far more quickly than he had expected, he heard a shot, then two shots, in rapid succession, and he knew that Bill's ammunition was gone. He heard a great outcry of snarls and yelps. Then the snarls ceased, and the yelping died away. Silence settled down again over the lonely land. Henry knew that the wolves had gotten Bill.

Henry sat for a long time before taking his ax from the sled. The two remaining dogs crouched and trembled at his feet.

He hastened to make a camp, gathering a generous supply of firewood. He fed the dogs, ate his supper, and made his bed close to the fire. Before his eyes had closed, the wolves had drawn too near for safety. He could not risk sleep.

By morning he was haggard and worn. He began the task he had thought about all night long. "They got Bill, an' they may get me, but they'll sure never get you," he said, addressing the dead body in the coffin as he heaved it up onto a tree-grave that he built from saplings.

Then he returned to the trail. He knew that if he could get to Fort McGurry, he would be safe.

With nightfall came more horror. The starving wolves grew bolder. Henry fought them off during the night by throwing burning cinders at them. When he grew tired, he tried to sleep holding on to fiery pine knots.

It worked until he closed his eyes momentarily and the pine fell away from his hand. The she-wolf was less than a yard away. Snarling and yelping, the wolves rushed toward him. Henry jumped toward the fire.

His face was blistering in the heat. His eyebrows and lashes were singed off, and the heat was becoming unbearable to his feet. The wolves had been driven back by the flames, but his two dogs were missing.

He stayed as close to the fire as he could. Then the she-wolf sat down, pointed her nose at a star, and began

to howl. One by one the wolves joined
her, until the whole pack of wolves sat
on their haunches, with noses pointing
skyward, and howled their hunger cry.

"I guess you can come an' get me,"
he mumbled. "I'm goin' to sleep."

Once, in a daze, Henry opened his
eyes and saw that a mysterious change
had taken place. The shock brought
him to full awareness. The wolves that
had almost got him were gone!

He heard men's voices cry out. Four

sleds pulled in from the riverbed to his camp among the trees. Half a dozen men were surrounding Henry, prodding him to wake up.

"A red she-wolf came in with the dogs at feedin' time," Henry said. "First she ate the dog-food. Then she ate the dogs. And after that she ate Bill."

"Where's Lord Alfred?" one of the men asked, shaking him roughly.

Henry shook his head slowly. "No, she didn't eat him. He's roostin' in a tree at the last camp."

"Dead?" the man shouted.

Exhausted, Henry nodded his head as if to say "yes," and fell asleep.

Far away, the cry of the hungry wolf pack could be heard as it followed the trail for more meat.

CHAPTER 4

The Battle of the Fangs

It was the she-wolf who first heard the sound of men's voices and the whining of the sled dogs. She was the first to jump away from the dying man and to lead the pack into the forest.

Another large gray wolf directed the pack's course on the heels of the she-wolf. He ran steadily just behind her, keeping a distance so she wouldn't snap at him. If he got too close, she would snarl and show her teeth. When she did, he never became angry with her.

The she-wolf had the large gray wolf on one side and a gaunt old wolf on the other side. This old wolf was grizzled and marked with the scars of many long battles. He had one eye only, the left eye, which was why he favored being on the she-wolf's right side.

Whenever she had to, the she-wolf fended off the attentions of both wolves with her teeth. As they searched for food, their rivalry for her attention became second to their hunger.

They ran many miles that day and all through the night. The next day they were still running. They ran over the surface of a dead, frozen world. They were alive, and they sought other

things that were alive. It was the way of the Wild.

The wolves stopped when a big bull moose appeared in their path. The pack attacked the bull from every side. He went down after a valiant struggle.

Now there was plenty of food, almost twenty pounds of meat for each of the wolves in the pack. When they were done, hardly a bone remained. With full stomachs, the wolves rested and slept. After a few days, they broke up and went off in separate groups, since now they had found herd after herd of moose.

With the young leader on her left and the one-eyed elder on her right, the she-wolf led their half of the pack down to the Mackenzie River. Then they crossed into the lake country to the east.

Every day, their number decreased as males and females went off in pairs. In the end, there remained only four: the she-wolf, the young leader, the one-eyed elder, and an eager three-year-old.

By now, the she-wolf had developed a ferocious temper. Her three suitors all bore the marks of her teeth. Yet they never defended themselves against her.

One day, in a fierce battle, the one-eyed elder and the young leader killed the three-year-old. Then the elder and the young leader fought, too. The elder wolf was a wise fighter. He took the young leader by surprise, sinking his fangs into the young leader's neck.

The young leader snarled terribly, but after such a blow he grew weaker and died. The she-wolf sat on her haunches, watching. For the first time, she was receptive to the elder wolf. She sniffed noses with him.

They ran through the woods, like good friends that have come to an understanding. As the days passed, they hunted and ate their meat together. After a time, the she-wolf grew restless. She seemed to be searching for something. The hollows under fallen trees

attracted her. She nosed among the larger snow-piled crevices in the rocks and in the caves of overhanging banks. Old One Eye was not interested at all, but he followed her good-naturedly.

One moonlit night, while running through the forest, One Eye suddenly stopped. His muzzle went up, his tail stiffened, and his nostrils dilated as he sniffed the air. He looked around warily, but his mate trotted on. Though he tried to follow her, he was still unsure.

She crept out cautiously on the edge of a large, open space in the midst of the trees. For some time, she stood alone. Then One Eye, creeping and crawling, his every sense on the alert, joined her. The two wolves stood side by side, watching and listening.

One Eye didn't know what was before him, but the she-wolf did. She seemed to know the ways of these men. It was an Indian camp—a perfect place to steal some food. Between them, the she-wolf and One Eye devoured all of the game they could find.

CHAPTER 5
The Cave

For two days the she-wolf and One Eye stayed near the camp, just out of sight. One Eye was wary, yet the camp lured his mate. When a rifle shot almost hit One Eye, they ran into the forest.

They did not go far. The she-wolf had gotten very heavy, and ran slowly. Her temper was short, and she snarled with impatience. As if to compensate for her distress, One Eye had become more gentle and patient.

Then she found a small cave tucked under the melting snowbanks. She inspected it while One Eye stood in the entrance and watched her. She dropped her head and lay down.

Old One Eye was hungry, but his mate didn't want to leave the cave. He went up the frozen bed of the stream. There he found some snowshoe rabbits, but they escaped him.

When he arrived back at the cave, he paused at the mouth. He heard faint sounds coming from within. He crawled carefully inside on his belly. The she-wolf snarled, so he kept his distance. He did not want to anger her.

Near her body, he saw five strange little bundles of life. The cubs were weak and helpless, with eyes that did not open to the light. They made tiny whimpering sounds. Even though One Eye had been a father before, he was still curious about these newborns.

His mate looked at him anxiously. She knew that wolf fathers could eat helpless newborn cubs, but this time there was no danger of that.

One Eye felt an impulse that was, in turn, an instinct that had come down to

him from all the wolf fathers. He did not question it. He knew, from the fiber of his being, that it was time to go on the trail of the meat.

Five or six miles from the cave, One Eye saw a porcupine. He began to draw closer to it. When it rolled into a ball with it quills sticking out, he knew not to go near it.

He went farther upstream and found a ptarmigan. When he came out of a thicket, he stood face to face with the slow-witted bird. He caught it and turned to return home with the bird. On the way back, he saw that a lynx was hunting the porcupine.

In that instant, the lynx attacked. Its rigid claws struck the underbelly of the porcupine, but not before the porcupine was able to sink its tail quills into the lynx's paw.

The porcupine's quills were in the lynx's nose. The lynx couldn't brush them away. In a frenzy of pain, the lynx

ran into the woods.

One Eye turned the porcupine over on its back. It didn't move. He began to drag the dead animal and then remembered the ptarmigan. He decided to eat the ptarmigan, then he returned to the cave with the porcupine.

CHAPTER 6

The Gray Cub

He was different from his brothers and sisters. He was the only gray cub in the litter and resembled his father.

Long before the gray cub's eyes had opened, he had learned by touch, taste, and smell to know his mother. She was a source of warmth, milk, and tenderness. She possessed a gentle, caressing tongue that soothed him when it passed over his soft little body. This feeling impelled him to snuggle close against her and to doze off to sleep.

After a few months he could see well. He began to romp with his brothers and sisters in a feeble, awkward way. He even began to growl a little as he

became accustomed to the movement.

The cave was gloomy. He did not know this, for he knew no other world. It was dimly lit, but his eyes had never had to adjust themselves to any other light. His world was very small. Its limits were the walls of the cave.

He discovered that one wall of his world was different from the rest. This was the mouth of the cave. He yearned to move toward the light that filtered in through the opening, but his mother kept him away with her paw or her muzzle, sometimes harshly.

He learned how it felt to be hurt and how to avoid being hurt. He was a fierce little cub. So were his brothers and sisters. He came from a breed of meat-killers and meat-eaters. He was the fiercest and most curious of the litter. As a result, he was the most difficult to keep from the mouth of the cave.

The light fascinated him. He did not know it marked an entrance or passage, but his instincts told him that it was the only way out.

The gray cub was not given to thinking, at least not the way people do. His brain worked in dim ways. Yet his conclusions were as sharp and distinct as those achieved by men. He was never disturbed over why a thing happened. Knowing that it happened was sufficient for him. Thus, when he had bumped his nose on the back wall of the cave a few times, he accepted that he could not walk through walls like his father seemed to do.

Like most creatures of the Wild, the gray cub experienced famine. It caused the deaths of his brothers and sisters. One Eye and the she-wolf did everything they could to find meat. Then a time came when the gray cub no longer saw his father. The she-wolf knew One Eye had been killed in a fierce battle with the lynx, whose cave was on the left fork of the river.

After that, the she-wolf avoided the left fork. She knew it was too risky to fight with a mean-tempered lynx that had kittens to feed. But the she-wolf was also a mother. When her cub's hunger increased and food became scarcer, she had no choice. To feed her child, she would risk anything.

CHAPTER 7

The World Beyond
the Cave

By the time his mother began leaving the cave to hunt, the cub knew not to follow. The she-wolf had taught her son well. If he obeyed, he would not encounter the dangers of the world beyond the cave.

But as he grew, the urge to explore beyond the mouth of the cave increased. When his mother went hunting, the cub was tempted to follow.

One day he drew very close to the mouth of the cave. The light was so bright that it blinded him. Beyond the wall stood trees that fringed the stream. A mountain towered above the trees, and the sky soared above the mountain.

The cub was afraid, but he moved forward. Nothing happened. He crouched at the lip of the cave. When he took another step, he tumbled forward. He yelped like a frightened puppy.

He rolled along the dry clay that lined the mouth of the cave. At last he came to a stop. He gave one last agonized yell and then a long, whimpering wail. Then he licked away the dry clay that now covered his body.

He sat up and gazed in wonder, like

an explorer in a new world. A squirrel running around the base of a tree trunk scared him. He cowered and snarled, but the squirrel was scared, too. It ran up the tree. From a point of safety, it chattered back savagely. This gave the cub courage.

Next he met a woodpecker and a moosebird. He reached out with a playful paw to touch the moosebird, but it pecked him on the nose and flew away.

The cub was learning that there were things that moved like he did and things that did not. He learned to be prepared and to expect the unexpected.

Although he was clumsy, the cub was getting a sense of the ground beneath him. He was learning to calculate his own muscular movements and to know his physical limitations. He was learning to measure distances between objects and himself.

Born to be a hunter, he stumbled upon meat just outside his own cave door on his first foray into the world. He fell right into a ptarmigan nest and discovered seven ptarmigan chicks. He ate the chicks. Then he licked his chops in the same way his mother did, and crawled out of the bush—right into the angry wings of the mother ptarmigan!

The mother ptarmigan was furious. At first the cub hid his head between his paws and yelped, but then he became angry. It was his first battle. He became fearless. He was fighting this live thing that was meat, and he was hungry.

The mother bird was stronger than he was. He retreated after getting pecked again and again. He lay down to rest near the edge of the bushes, his tongue out, his chest heaving, his nose still sore.

As he rested, the cub suddenly had a feeling of dread. The unknown with all its terrors rushed upon him. He shrank back, instinctively, into the shelter of the bush. As he did so, a draft of air

fanned him, and a large, winged body swept ominously and silently past. A hawk, driving down out of the blue, barely missed him.

While he lay in the bush, the cub saw the swift downward swoop of the hawk. It grabbed the ptarmigan in its talons and carried it away. It was an important lesson for the cub: Danger could come from anywhere at any time.

A long time passed before the cub left its shelter in the bush again. He had learned a lot. Live things were meat. They were good to eat. Also, live things, when they were large enough, could hurt him. It was better to eat small live things like ptarmigan chicks, and to leave big live things alone.

When he was ready to try again, the cub boldly stepped into a stream. He was surprised when he fell into it. After much paddling and splashing, he was able to swim to the bank and rest. He would be more careful next time.

The gray cub moved on. He wanted to return to the cave. Then he came upon a baby weasel and its mother. The weasel mother bit his shoulder. While he yelped and scrambled backward, the mother weasel moved her baby to safety. The cub quickly learned that the mother weasel, although small, was one of the most savage opponents in the Wild.

The weasel came closer to the gray cub. The cub would have been killed, and there would have been no story to write about him. But just then the she-

wolf bounded through the bushes to free her cub from the weasel's grip. The she-wolf killed the mother weasel. Then, the she-wolf nuzzled her cub and licked his wounds. After eating the mother weasel, they went back to the cave and slept.

CHAPTER 8

Eat, or Be Eaten

The cub grew quickly. Every day he explored a wider area, discovering when to be bold and when to be cautious.

His desire to kill for meat strengthened as the days passed. He learned that the squirrel's chatter informed all wild creatures that the wolf cub was approaching. But as birds flew in the air, squirrels could climb trees. To attack the squirrel, the cub could only try to crawl, unobserved, up to the squirrel when it was on the ground.

The cub respected his mother. She always brought him his share of meat, she was brave, and she was powerful. She no longer corrected him with her paw or a nudge of her nose, but with the slash of her fangs.

Food became scarce again. Once more, the cub felt hunger gnawing at his belly. The she-wolf rarely slept in her quest for meat. This famine was not long, but it was severe. Now the cub began to hunt in earnest, no longer in play, but he found nothing. Still, this added to his growing skills.

He learned to catch squirrels and wood mice. He also learned about the

ways of moosebirds and woodpeckers.

One day, the hawk's shadow no longer drove him crouching into the bushes. He had grown stronger and more confident.

In desperation, he sat on his haunches in the open and challenged the hawk to come down from the sky. He knew that there, floating in the blue above him, was food. But the hawk refused to come down and fight with him, so the cub crawled away into a thicket and whimpered to himself.

The famine broke when the she-wolf brought home a lynx kitten. It was all for him. His mother had already eaten the rest of the lynx litter, which was a desperate deed.

With his stomach full, the cub lay in the cave against his mother's side. He woke up to the most ferocious snarling he had ever heard. The lynx mother stood at the opening of the cave.

The cub stood by his mother's side

and snarled. Together, they fought the
lynx. Although the lynx was killed, the
she-wolf and the cub were injured in
the fight. The she-wolf was very weak
and sick. She licked the cub's wounds,
and then lay for a full day and night
near her dead foe's side.

For a week, she only left the cave for
water. Her movements were slow and
painful. At the end of that time, they
devoured the lynx. When the she-wolf's
wounds had healed, she went out again

on the trail of meat.

The cub's shoulder was stiff and sore from the bites and slashes he had received. For some time, he limped. But even so, now the world seemed changed to him. He had more confidence. He had buried his teeth in the flesh of an enemy and he had survived.

He began to hunt with his mother and to learn the law of survival: Eat, or be eaten.

After this primary law, there were

lesser laws for him to learn and obey. The world was filled with surprises. To have a full stomach and to doze lazily in the sunshine made him happy. The gray cub was very much alive, very happy, and very proud of himself.

CHAPTER 9

The Makers of Fire

The cub got his first glimpse of humans by accident when he was going to the stream for a drink. By the bank sat five Indian men. They didn't move when they saw him. The cub didn't move when he saw the men.

For the first time, the cub felt an instinct that conflicted with every other he had ever had. He felt an overwhelming sense of his own weakness. Somehow, he knew that men had mastery and power.

Had he been full-grown, he would have run away. Small and alone as he was, he froze and cowered in fear. One of the Indians approached the cub and reached down to take hold of him.

When the cub bared his teeth, the men laughed.

"Look! The white fangs!" one said.

The cub felt two great impulses at once—to yield and to fight. Torn and indecisive, he did both, snapping his jaws around the man's hand.

The man hit him on the side of his head and knocked him over. The cub sat up and yelped, but the man whose hand he had bitten was angry. The man hit him on the other side of his head. He sat up and yelped louder than ever.

Once again, the men laughed. The cub saw his mother coming to protect him. She was snarling.

"Kiche! She ran way a year ago!" said one of the men.

Then the she-wolf stopped when she heard her name. The cub crouched near his mother.

"She has lived with the wolves," said a third Indian.

"So it would seem, Three Eagles,"

Gray Beaver answered, putting his hand on the cub. "And this is the sign of it."

The cub snarled at the man's touch, and the hand flew back to slap him on the snout. The cub covered its fangs and sank down submissively, while the hand, returning, rubbed gently behind his ears and up and down his back.

"It is plain that his mother is Kiche and his father was a wolf. His fangs are white, and White Fang shall be his name. I have spoken. He is my dog," Gray Beaver said.

The cub watched as Gray Beaver took his knife, cut a stick, and used rawhide to tie Kiche to a pine tree. White Fang followed and lay down beside her. He hated to be handled by these men, but he could do nothing to defend himself. So he stayed with his mother.

Soon the entire tribe arrived. White Fang saw many men, women, children, and dogs. The people and the dogs carried heavy packs of supplies. White

Fang had never seen dogs before. He watched quietly and curiously.

They rushed upon him, biting and snapping. Some of the men drove back the dogs, so White Fang stood up again. The men protected White Fang by throwing sticks and stones at the dogs.

When the last dog had been driven back, the uproar died down. White Fang licked his wounds and thought about what had just happened. This was his first taste of pack cruelty. He

was angry and confused that his own kind had tried to destroy him and that his mother was tied with a stick.

For a long time the Indians' tepees frightened White Fang until he got used to them. He strayed from his mother and met a somewhat larger and older puppy. It came toward him slowly.

The puppy's name was Lip-lip. He was a bully. White Fang approached him in a friendly way. But when the

stranger's walk became stiff-legged and his lips lifted clear of his teeth, White Fang stiffened, too.

Suddenly, with remarkable swiftness, Lip-lip leaped across the ground. Before White Fang knew it, an opponent who deserved to be feared was attacking him. Lip-lip relentlessly slashed and snapped, while White Fang dodged each move as best he could.

It was the first of many fights between the two animals. Their natures clashed, and there was nothing that White Fang could do to make living in the camp, while Lip-lip was around, less strained. It was yet another lesson that White Fang had to learn. There were those, men and animals, who would seek to hurt him. He must be ever on his guard against them.

Later, when Gray Beaver was making a fire, White Fang became curious. He moved slowly toward the fire, trying to investigate. When he came too close to the flames, White Fang burned his nose and tongue. It was the worst pain he had yet experienced. Adding to his torment was the sound of laughter that greeted his pain. Everyone in the camp was laughing at him.

White Fang hung his head in shame. He was angry and confused. He longed for the quiet of the stream and the comfort of the cave. He had been protected there and could learn slowly. Now, without the protection of his mother and the companionship of the other cubs, he was alone with these strange men and animals.

From a distance, White Fang watched the men. White Fang knew that they were to be feared and obeyed. They were fire-makers. They had power.

CHAPTER 10

The Indian Camp

White Fang quickly learned the ways of the camp. He knew the injustice and greed of the older dogs when meat or fish was thrown to them. He learned that men were more just, children more cruel, and women more kind and more likely to toss him a bit of meat or bone. He learned to stay away from the dog mothers with puppies to protect.

While Kiche was restrained by the stick, White Fang explored the camp. The more he came to know them, the more he understood the Indians. Just as his mother had responded to them from the first cry of her name, he was also beginning to answer to their calls.

When they approached, he got out of their way. When they called, he came. When they threatened, he cowered. Behind their commands was the power to enforce those commands. Their power was expressed by clubs, flying stones, and stinging lashes of whips.

Now he belonged to them. He depended on them. It seemed easier this way. This happened slowly since White Fang could not immediately forget his memories of the Wild.

While White Fang avoided many of the dangers of his new life with the Indians, he could not avoid Lip-lip. The big puppy tormented White Fang, and White Fang suffered.

White Fang was an outcast among the puppies. To get his share of food, he became a clever thief. He learned to sneak around the camp and to know what was going on everywhere.

White Fang once got the better of Lip-lip by tricking him. As Lip-lip chased

White Fang around a corner, he ran into the raging jaws of Kiche. She pushed him down so that he could not run, while she repeatedly ripped and slashed him with her fangs. White Fang rushed in and sank his teeth into Lip-lip's hind leg. After that, there was no fight left in Lip-lip, and he ran back to his own tepee.

In the Wild, a mother's time with her young is short. Under the dominion of man, it is sometimes even shorter.

A day came when Gray Beaver gave Kiche to Three Eagles. When White Fang saw his mother taken aboard Three Eagles's canoe, he jumped into the water to follow. Three Eagles struck White Fang to chase him back to land. Then the canoe moved away from the bank. White Fang still followed.

Gray Beaver went after White Fang in his canoe. He lifted White Fang out of the water and beat him. At first, White Fang was surprised, then afraid, then angry. He showed his teeth and snarled. Gray Beaver hit White Fang even harder.

When the canoe reached the shore, White Fang crawled to his feet and stood whimpering. Lip-lip had been watching from the bank. Now he rushed upon White Fang, knocking him over and sinking his teeth into his enemy. White Fang was too helpless to defend himself, but Gray Beaver kicked Lip-lip into the air.

This was man's form of justice. Even in his pitiable state, White Fang felt a grateful thrill. Obediently, he limped along at Gray Beaver's heels through the village to the tepee.

White Fang's life was not entirely unhappy. He found much to interest him in the village. He learned how to get along with Gray Beaver. If he obeyed his master, he was not beaten.

Gray Beaver sometimes tossed White Fang a piece of meat, and he defended him against the other dogs when they jumped in to eat it. A piece of meat from Gray Beaver was of great value. In some strange way, it was worth more than a dozen pieces of meat from the hand of one woman, even though Gray Beaver never petted or caressed him.

White Fang became more and more ferocious and shrewd in confronting Lip-lip. He was an outcast in camp among the people and the dogs. All of the young dogs followed Lip-lip's lead. There was a difference between White

Fang and them. He was from the Wild. They instinctively hated him for it.

From their harsh treatment, White Fang learned how to take care of himself in a group fight and how to inflict the greatest damage to a single dog in the briefest amount of time. He became cat-like in his ability to stay on his feet.

Unlike other dogs, he never wasted time at the beginning of a fight by snarling, bristling, or strutting. He rushed in and snapped and slashed, before his opponent had a chance to prepare for battle.

He also made sure that none of them could venture out alone without worrying that he would attack. They had made a fierce enemy of him. Except for Lip-lip, they were forced to hunch together for protection against him. He was both the hunter and the hunted.

CHAPTER 11

Under the Protection of Men

In the fall, White Fang got his chance for liberty. For several days there had been a great hubbub in the village. The camp was being dismantled as the tribe prepared to leave for the fall hunting. White Fang watched the canoes disappear down the river.

He was determined to stay behind. He waited for his opportunity to slip out of the camp to the woods and hide. Then he heard Gray Beaver call him. White Fang trembled. He felt the urge to crawl out of his hiding place, but he resisted it. Later, he crept out and was free!

He played in the darkness for a while, but began to feel lonely. The dark forest

and hovering trees frightened him. He was cold, and there was no warm tepee to lean against. The frost stung his feet. He curved his bushy tail around his feet to keep them warm.

At the same time, he saw a vision of the camp, the people, the warm fire, and the pieces of meat and fish that had been thrown to him.

His experience as a captive had weakened him. He had forgotten how to fend for himself. He ran toward the village, but no village greeted his eyes. The village had gone away.

He came to the place where Gray Beaver's tepee had stood. In the center of the space it had occupied, he sat down. He pointed his nose at the moon. A heartbroken cry bubbled up from his loneliness, his grief for Kiche, all his past sorrows and miseries, and his fear of what was to come. It was the first howl he had ever uttered.

His fears faded with the coming of

daylight, but he was still lonely. He plunged into the forest and followed the river downstream. All day he ran. His iron-like body went on, even after fatigue came.

White Fang ran all night, then for two more days. After thirty hours his strength began to give out. He had not eaten, and he was weak with hunger.

Had it not been for Gray Beaver's wife, Kloo-kooch, White Fang would have died or become a wild wolf until the end of his

days. She had seen a moose, which Gray Beaver had shot, forcing them to set up a camp near the riverbank.

Sounds from the camp reached White Fang. He saw the blaze of the fire, Klookooch cooking, and Gray Beaver squatting near the fire. There was fresh meat in the camp!

White Fang expected to be beaten. He crouched and bristled a little. Then he went forward again. He wanted the comfort of the fire, the protection of the men, and even the companionship of the dogs. He would risk the beating.

He crawled into the firelight. Gray Beaver saw him and stopped eating. White Fang crawled slowly toward Gray Beaver, every inch of his progress becoming slower and more painful. At last, he lay at his master's feet.

White Fang trembled, waiting for his punishment. The hand above him moved. He stole a glance upward. Gray Beaver was offering him a piece of meat!

Very gently and somewhat suspiciously, White Fang smelled the meat and then ate it. Gray Beaver ordered more meat to be brought to White Fang, and he guarded him from the other dogs while he ate. Grateful and content, White Fang lay at Gray Beaver's feet, gazing at the fire that warmed him.

CHAPTER 12

Food in Exchange
for Freedom

I n December, Gray Beaver went on a
journey up the Mackenzie River. He
took his son, Mit-sah, and Kloo-kooch.

Mit-sah drove a second smaller sled,
pulled by a team of puppies. He was
learning to drive and train dogs, while
the puppies were being broken in to
the harness. The sled carried nearly
two hundred pounds of supplies.

White Fang had seen the camp dogs
toiling in the harness, so when the harness was placed on him he did not
mind. The dogs were tied to the sled so
that none would trod in another's footsteps. The dog behind could never catch
up with the one in front, but the dogs

ran fast to try to catch one another.

Mit-sah noticed how Lip-lip tormented White Fang. He harnessed Lip-lip as
the lead dog. Now all of the other dogs
hated Lip-lip and chased him. Because
Lip-lip was at the end of the longest
rope, the dogs always saw him running
away. This made him seem less ferocious.

White Fang worked hard. He was
faithful and willing. These are traits of
the wolf and the wild dog when they
have become domesticated. White Fang
had these traits in great measure.

White Fang had no companionship
with the dogs. He only knew how to fight
with them. He snapped and slashed at
them the way they did when Lip-lip was
their leader.

With Lip-lip's overthrow, White Fang
could have become the pack leader. But
he was too much of a loner. He either
thrashed his teammates or ignored
them. None of them would steal his

meat. They ate as quickly as they could for fear that White Fang would take their food. White Fang knew well the law of survival: Oppress the weak and obey the strong.

As the months passed, White Fang's strength grew, due to the long hours on the trail and the steady toil at the sled. For him, the world was fierce and brutal.

He had no love for Gray Beaver, who was a harsh master. Gray Beaver did not pet or speak kind words. He ruled with a club. He showed his kindness by withholding a blow.

So White Fang knew nothing of the pleasure of a stroke from a man's hand. To White Fang, men's hands were dangerous. Men threw stones and wielded sticks, clubs, and whips. He stayed away from children, too, who pinched and grabbed.

One day, while Mit-sah was gathering firewood in the forest, a boy attacked him. When White Fang realized that it

was Mit-sah who was being mistreated, White Fang bit the other boy. White Fang knew he had committed a serious crime, but Gray Beaver didn't punish him. He gave White Fang extra meat that night for protecting Mit-sah.

After this happened, Gray Beaver trained White Fang to be even more ferocious and more solitary. The bond between White Fang and Gray Beaver grew stronger.

The terms of their bond were simple.

To live among men, White Fang exchanged his own liberty. Food, fire, protection, and companionship were some of the things he received from Gray Beaver. In return, he guarded Gray Beaver's property, defended his family, worked for him, and obeyed him.

White Fang's was a service of duty and awe, but not of love. Eventually, his allegiance to man would outweigh his love of liberty, of kind, and of kin.

CHAPTER 13

The Famine

It was April when Gray Beaver finished his long journey. White Fang was a year old when he pulled into the home village and Mit-sah released him from the harness.

Although not fully grown yet, White Fang was the largest yearling in the village after Lip-lip. To all appearances, he was a true wolf. The quarter-strain of dog he inherited from Kiche left no mark on him physically, but it did play a part in his behavior toward men.

He wandered through the village and saw the people and dogs he had known before. Now he walked among them with a certain ease that was as new to him as it was enjoyable. White Fang had a new power over his teammates. He fought with the other dogs for his meat and won. He demanded the respect due to him. The other dogs quickly learned to leave him alone.

In midsummer, White Fang returned from a hunting trip and ran directly into Kiche. He vaguely remembered her. He bounded toward her, but she growled and snarled at him. He backed away.

It was not Kiche's fault. A wolf-mother

is not made to remember her cubs from a year or so before. White Fang was a strange animal, an intruder. Kiche had a new litter of puppies to protect.

When one of the puppies crawled up to White Fang and he sniffed it, Kiche attacked him. The third time she attacked, White Fang allowed himself to be driven away. It was the law of his kind that males must not fight females. He knew this by instinct. This was the same way he knew to howl at the moon and stars at night and to fear death and the unknown.

As the months went by, Gray Beaver prized White Fang more. White Fang's only weakness was that he hated to be laughed at. If someone laughed at him, he became ferocious.

In the third year of his life there was a great famine. Only the strongest members of their tribe survived. White Fang, like many of the other dogs, fled to the woods. He was better fitted to survive on

his own than the other dogs were, for he had the training of his cubhood to guide him. He was a good hunter.

Fortune favored White Fang. When hardest pressed for food, he found something to kill. Early in the summer, during the last days of the famine, he met Lip-lip, who had also gone into to the woods. They rounded a corner of rock and found themselves face to face.

White Fang was in splendid condition. His hunting had been good, and for a week he had eaten his fill. Lip-lip had found little food and was weak. Lip-lip tried to back away, but White Fang struck him hard, shoulder-to-shoulder. The wounded dog rolled on his back. White Fang's teeth drove into the scrawny throat. Lip-lip was defeated.

Weeks passed. Then one day, White Fang came to the edge of the forest and found a village. He smelled food. He boldly came out from the forest and trotted into the camp, straight up to

Gray Beaver's tepee. Gray Beaver was not there, but Kloo-kooch welcomed him with freshly caught fish. After he had eaten, White Fang lay down to wait for Gray Beaver.

An Enemy of His Kind

When White Fang became leader of the sled-team, the other dogs hated him more than ever. They hated him for the extra meat Mit-sah gave him and for all of the other favors he received. His waving brush of a tail and retreating hindquarters running before them maddened them, too.

White Fang hated them, as well. Being sled-leader and having to run away in front of the yelling pack of dogs that had been afraid of him was almost more than he could endure. He developed a hatred that was as ferocious as his nature. His reputation spread to many villages.

When White Fang was nearly five years old, Gray Beaver took him on another journey. He encountered and fought with many dogs in all of the villages. They had no chance against him. If a dog bit him, it was by accident. He went unscratched because he was such an efficient fighter.

In the summer of 1898, White Fang arrived at Fort Yukon with Gray Beaver. They went to the old Hudson's Bay Company Fort. There were many

Indians, a lot of food, and much activity. Thousands of gold hunters were going up the Yukon to Dawson and the Klondike. Many had been traveling for more than a year and still had far to go. Some came from five thousand miles away, while others came from the other side of the world.

Gray Beaver stopped at Fort Yukon to sell and trade his wares. There White Fang saw white men for the first time. They were more powerful than the Indians. Their houses and the huge fort, made of massive logs, looked very different from the Indian tepees.

White Fang was an object of great curiosity to the men at the fort. His wolfish appearance caught their eyes at once. Their attention put White Fang on his guard. When they tried to approach him, he bared his teeth and backed away. Not one white man succeeded in laying a hand on him, and it was well that they did not.

If the white men were all-powerful, their dogs did not amount to much. None of the dogs knew how to fight.

White Fang enjoyed fighting with them. They were soft from years of domestication. It was the dogs' instinct to attack White Fang as soon as they saw him. He was from the Wild—the unknown, the terrible.

There was one man among the white men at Fort Yukon who particularly enjoyed watching White Fang defeat the other dogs. He admired White Fang's cunning. One day, he hoped, this brave dog would be his.

This man was known in the country as Beauty Smith. No one knew his real first name. Beauty Smith was anything but handsome. He was known far and wide as a sniveling coward.

Men tolerated and feared him. His cowardly rages made them dread a shot in the back or poison in their coffee. But somebody had to do the cooking, and

Beauty Smith could cook.

Smith was delighted by White Fang's ferocious nature. He tried to get near White Fang, but White Fang bristled, bared his teeth, and backed away. He did not like the man.

Smith tried to buy White Fang. At first Gray Beaver refused to sell the dog, but when his money ran out, he agreed. One night, when White Fang returned to the camp, Gray Beaver placed a leather collar around his neck. An hour later, Smith strode into camp and stood over him. White Fang snarled softly, watching the man's hands.

When Smith reached out to touch him, White Fang snapped, striking with his fangs like a snake. Smith jerked back his hand before White Fang's teeth came together with a sharp click. Smith was frightened and angry. Gray Beaver smacked White Fang on the side of his head.

White Fang's suspicious eyes followed

every move Smith made. When Smith returned with a club, Gray Beaver handed Smith the leather leash. Smith started to walk away. The thong grew taut. White Fang resisted it. Gray Beaver hit him right and left to make him get up and follow. He didn't obey, so Smith hit him with the club.

Finally, White Fang followed at Smith's heels, his tail between his legs. He snarled softly under his breath.

CHAPTER 15

White Fang
Learns to Hate

Under Smith's command, White Fang became a fiend. He was chained in a pen at the rear of the fort. Smith tormented him. He knew White Fang hated being laughed at, so he laughed at White Fang constantly.

White Fang was enraged and became more ferocious than ever. He hated the chain that bound him and the men who peered at him through the slats of the pen. He hated the dogs that accompanied the men and snarled at him in his helplessness. He hated the very wood of the pen that confined him. Most of all, he hated Beauty Smith.

Smith wanted White Fang to become

fierce and brutal. Smith earned money
when the men placed bets to see which
dog would win. Strangely, White Fang
came to look forward to these fights. It
was the only time he could satisfy the
hatred he had developed for his captor.

One day, three dogs turned on him in
succession. Another day, a full-grown
wolf was placed in the pen, and on
another day two dogs at the same time.
This was his severest fight, and although
in the end he killed them both, White
Fang was half-killed.

In the fall of the year, Smith took passage for himself and White Fang on a
steamboat bound up the Yukon to
Dawson. White Fang had now achieved
a reputation in the land. He was known
as the "Fighting Wolf."

The mere sight of Smith drove White
Fang into a fury. No matter how terribly
he was beaten, White Fang always had
another growl; and when Beauty Smith
gave up and withdrew, White Fang's

defiant growl followed him, or White Fang sprang at the bars of the cage bellowing his hatred.

When the steamboat arrived at Dawson, White Fang went ashore and fought dog after dog. As the time went by, he had fewer and fewer fights. Men despaired of matching him with an animal that was his equal. Smith was compelled to pit wolves against him. Once, a full-grown female lynx was secured, and this time White Fang fought for his life. Her quickness matched his, and he was forced to fight both fang and claw.

After White Fang defeated the lynx, there were no more animals to fight. That is, until Tim Keenan arrived with the first bulldog, named Cherokee, that had ever entered the Klondike.

Smith slipped the chain from White Fang's neck and stepped back. For the first time, White Fang did not make an immediate attack. He stood still, with his ears pricked forward, alert and curi-

ous, watching the strange animal that faced him.

Keenan shoved the bulldog forward and muttered, "Go to it." The animal was short and squat. It waddled toward the center of the circle, came to a stop, and blinked at White Fang.

From the crowd there were cries of "Go to him, Cherokee! Sick 'em, Cherokee! Eat 'em up!"

White Fang struck. A cry of startled admiration went up. He had covered the distance and gone in more like a cat than a dog and, with the same cat-like swiftness, he had slashed with his fangs and leaped clear.

Cherokee was bleeding. Again, and yet again, White Fang sprang in, slashed, and got away untouched, and still the bulldog followed him. He was waiting for a chance to get his teeth into White Fang. Because of the difference in their sizes, White Fang could not get a hold of the bulldog's throat.

For the first time in White Fang's fighting history, men saw him lose his footing. His body turned a half-somer-sault in the air. He would have landed on his back had he not twisted, cat-like, in the effort to bring his feet to the earth. He fell on his side and quickly regained his feet, but in the next instant, Cherokee's teeth closed on his throat.

Cherokee's bite was too low down toward the chest, but he held on. White Fang rolled wildly around, trying to

shake off the bulldog's body. This clinging, dragging weight made White Fang frantic. White Fang ceased only when he had tired himself out. Never, in all his fighting, had this happened. There was no escaping Cherokee's grip.

It began to look as though the battle was over. At last White Fang fell, exhausted. Then the bulldog shifted his grip, coming in closer, mangling more and more of the fur-folded flesh. Shouts of applause went up for the victor, and there were many cries of "Cherokee! Cherokee!"

Just then, a dog-musher's cries were heard. A sled pulled up with two men. The dog-musher wore a mustache. His name was Matt. The other, a taller and younger man, was smooth-shaven. His skin was rosy from the pounding of his blood and from running in the frosty air. His name was Weedon Scott.

White Fang was ready to give in. Smith saw White Fang's eyes beginning to glaze. Smith sprang upon White Fang and savagely kicked him.

Suddenly, Scott forced his way through the crowd. When he broke through into the ring, Smith was just about to kick White Fang again. At that moment the newcomer's fist struck Smith's face, knocking him to the ground. Smith's shock was apparent.

"You cowards!" Scott cried to the crowd. "You beasts! Come on, Matt, lend a hand," Scott called to the dog-musher, who had followed him into the ring.

Both men bent over the dogs. "You beasts!" Scott exploded against the men, trying to break the bulldog's grip.

"It's no use, Scott. You can't break 'em apart that way," Matt said.

The younger man's excitement and concern for White Fang was growing. Finally, the dogs were drawn apart. The bulldog struggled vigorously.

"Take him away," Scott commanded, and Keenan, Cherokee's owner, dragged Cherokee back into the crowd.

White Fang tried to get to his feet, but could not. "He's breathin' all right," Matt said, bending down to listen.

Smith had regained his feet and come over to look at White Fang.

"Matt, how much is a good sled-dog worth?" Scott asked.

"Three hundred dollars," Matt answered.

"And how much for one that's all chewed up like this one?" Scott asked, nudging White Fang with his foot.

"Half of that," was Matt's judgment. Scott turned to Smith. He opened his wallet and counted out the bills. Smith put his hands behind his back, refusing to touch the money.

"I ain't a-sellin'," he said.

"Oh yes, you are," Scott assured him. "Because I'm buying. Here's your money. The dog's mine. You gave up your rights to own that dog."

"All right," Smith conceded. He was afraid of being struck again. But then he added, "Wait until I get back to Dawson. I'll have the law on you."

"If you open your mouth, I'll have you run out of town. Understand?" Scott threatened.

Smith replied with a grunt.

Scott turned his back on him and returned to help the dog-musher, who was tending to White Fang. Some of the men were already departing; others stood in groups, watching and talking. Keenan joined one of the groups.

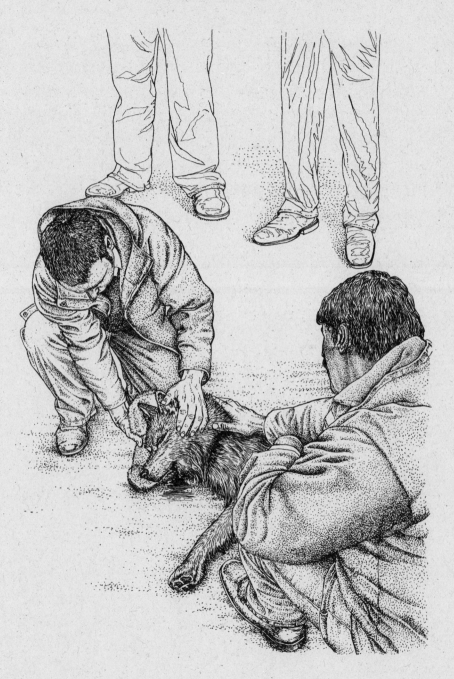

"Who's that guy?" Keenan asked.

"Weedon Scott," someone answered. "One of them mining experts. Got a lot of friends in high places. The gold commissioner's a friend of his."

"I thought he must be somebody," Keenan said. "That's why I kept my hands off him at the start."

CHAPTER 16

Taming the Beast

"It's hopeless," Scott sighed as he sat on the step outside the door of his cabin and stared at Matt, who gave a shrug.

They looked at White Fang. It had been two weeks, and he seemed more vicious than when the men had first saved him.

"It's a wolf and there's no taming it," Scott announced.

"Oh, I don't know about that," Matt objected. "Might be a lot of dog in him, for all you can tell. Looks like he's been trained to the harness. See those marks across his chest?"

"You're right, Matt. He was a sled-dog before Beauty Smith got him," Scott agreed.

"And there's not much reason against his bein' a sled-dog again."

It took a while for the men to find out that White Fang feared clubs and hated guns. He would cower when a man approached with a club, but became ferocious if he saw a gun.

Matt approached White Fang with a club in hand. When he got close he was able to unsnap the chain from the collar.

White Fang couldn't believe that he was free. He walked slowly and cautiously. He did not know what to do.

"Won't he run away?" his new owner asked.

Matt shrugged his shoulders. "Got to take a gamble. The only way to find out is to find out."

"Poor devil," Scott murmured. "What he needs is some human kindness." He got a piece of meat and tossed it to White Fang. The dog sprang away from the meat. From a distance, White Fang

studied it suspiciously.

Major, another dog, ran for the meat. Matt tried to stop White Fang's attack, but he was bitten in the clash.

Scott took out his revolver. "I'm going to have to kill him," he said.

"Look here, Mr. Scott," Matt objected, "that dog's been through a lot. You can't expect him to be gentle. Give him time."

"You know I don't want to kill him," Scott answered, putting away the revolver. "We'll let him run loose and see what kindness can do for him."

He walked over to White Fang and began talking to him soothingly. White Fang was suspicious. As Scott's hand touched his head, White Fang shrank. He snarled and crouched lower, and still the hand descended. He did not want to bite the hand, but he did.

Scott cried out sharply. Matt dashed into the cabin and came out with a rifle. Now it was Scott's turn to plead for White Fang's life.

"Look how smart he is," Scott said, seeing White Fang's reaction to Matt's rifle. "He knows the meaning of firearms as well as you do. He's intelligent, and we've got to give that intelligence a chance. Put the gun down."

Matt shook his head in agreement. He lowered the gun.

"You are right, Mr. Scott. That dog's much too intelligent to kill," he replied.

As White Fang watched Scott approach, he bristled and snarled. He expected a punishment. Instead, Scott

sat down several feet away.

White Fang stopped snarling. Then Scott spoke. At first, the sound of his voice made the fur rise on White Fang's neck. Scott went on calmly talking. For a time, White Fang growled in unison with him.

Scott talked softly and soothingly, with a gentleness that touched White Fang. In spite of the warnings of his instinct, White Fang began to have confidence in Scott. He had a feeling of security that belied all of his previous experience with men.

After a long time, Scott got up and went into the cabin. He came back and sat down as before, in the same spot, several feet away. He held out a small piece of meat.

White Fang's ears rose. He investigated the meat suspiciously, managing to look at the same time at the meat and Scott. His body tensed, ready to spring away at the first sign of danger.

Scott tossed the meat on the snow at
White Fang's feet. White Fang smelled
the meat carefully, but he did not look at
it. While he smelled it, he kept his eyes
on Scott. When nothing happened, he
took the meat into his mouth and swallowed it. Still nothing happened.

Scott offered him another piece of
meat. Again, White Fang refused to
take it from Scott's hand, and again it
was tossed to him. This was repeated a
number of times, but eventually Scott
refused to toss it.

The meat was good, and White Fang
was hungry. Bit by bit, he approached
the hand. Finally, he decided to eat the
meat. He never took his eyes from Scott,
thrusting his head forward with ears
flattened back and hair involuntarily ris-
ing and cresting on his neck. A low
growl rumbled in his throat as a warning. Piece by piece, he ate all of the meat
from Scott's hand.

Scott went on talking. In his voice

was kindness—something White Fang had never experienced. It aroused new feelings in White Fang.

Scott thrust his hand at White Fang. Despite the menacing hand, Scott's voice was gentle. White Fang snarled, bristled, and flattened his ears, but he neither snapped nor sprang away.

Nearer and nearer the hand came. It touched the ends of his upstanding hair. He shrank under it. It followed down after him, pressing more closely against him. Shrinking, almost shivering, White Fang still managed to hold himself together.

It was a torment, this hand that caressed him. He had been hurt from such a hand. He could never forget that.

CHAPTER 17

White Fang
Learns to Trust

Scott's hand lifted and descended again in a patting, caressing movement. White Fang growled. Matt came out of the cabin with a pan of dirty dishwater. He could not believe his eyes.

Matt's voice broke the silence. White Fang leaped back, snarling savagely at Matt. Scott smiled with a superior air, rose to his feet, and walked over to White Fang. He talked soothingly to the animal, but not for long. Then, slowly, he put out his hand, rested it on White Fang's head, and resumed patting. White Fang endured it, keeping his eyes fixed suspiciously on Matt.

Scott had gone to the roots of White

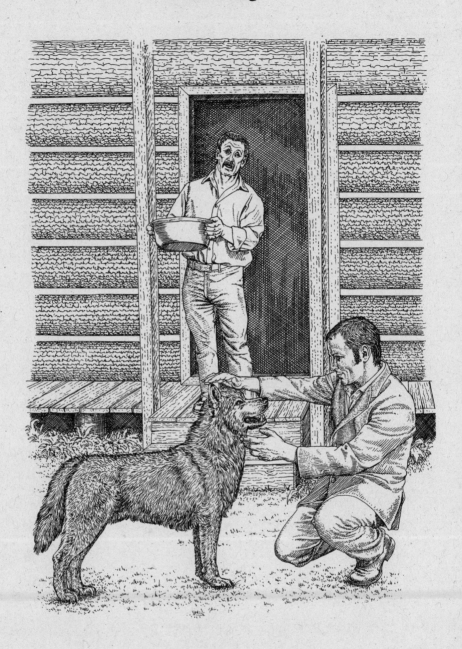

Fang's nature, and with kindness touched a part of him that had seemed dead. But trust came slowly. White Fang began to guard his master's property. He guarded the cabin while the sled dogs slept. Soon, he learned to detect the difference between cruel thieves and honest men.

Scott felt that the ill done to White Fang must be repaid. Each day, Scott made it a point to caress him.

White Fang grew to enjoy being petted. He growled when the hand touched him, but it was a growl with a new note in it. No one could hear that note except Scott.

White Fang's nature began to open up as a flower opens under the sun. He did not easily show his affection. He was used to harsh treatment, so it was hard for him to trust. Only by the steady regard of his eyes did he express his love for Scott.

White Fang came to tolerate Matt

because he was a possession of his master, and because Matt fed White Fang.

It was Matt who tried to put him into the harness and make him haul the sled with the other dogs. But Matt failed. It was not until Scott put the harness on White Fang and worked him that White Fang accepted it.

White Fang took it as his master's will that Matt should drive him and work him, just as Matt drove and worked the other dogs. But White Fang's loyalty was to Scott only.

Quickly, White Fang became the leader of the dogsled. The Klondike sleds with runners under them were different from the sleds that White Fang had pulled before. In the Klondike, the leader was, indeed, the leader—the wisest, as well as strongest, dog. The team obeyed him and feared him.

After he had worked on the sled during the day, White Fang guarded his master's property at night. He was on

duty all of the time. He was ever vigilant and faithful—the most valuable of all the dogs.

In the late spring, without warning, Scott left. Matt wrote to Scott about White Fang's sadness. Scott read the letter in Circle City, Alaska:

"That wolf won't work. Won't eat. He has no spunk left. All the dogs are licking him. Wants to know what has become of you, and I don't know how to tell him. Maybe he is going to die."

White Fang would not eat. He allowed the other dogs to thrash him. In the cabin, he lay on the floor near the stove, without interest in food, in Matt, or in life. White Fang never did more than turn his dull eyes upon the man. Then he would drop his head back on his forepaws.

One night, Matt was reading silently to himself. He was startled by a low whine from White Fang, who had risen to his feet, his ears cocked toward the

door. A moment later, Matt heard footsteps. The door opened, and Scott stepped in. The two men shook hands. Then Scott looked around the room.

"Where's the wolf?" he asked. Then Scott saw White Fang, standing where he had been lying, near the stove. White Fang did not rush forward. He stood, watching and waiting.

"Look at him wag his tail!" Matt exclaimed. Scott strode halfway across the room toward him, at the same time calling him. White Fang came to him, not with a great bound, yet quickly. As White Fang drew near, his eyes took on a strange expression.

"He never looked at me that way, all the time you were gone!" Matt said.

Scott was not listening. He was squatting down on his heels, face-to-face with White Fang, petting him. Scott rubbed at the roots of the ears, making long, caressing strokes down the neck to the shoulders, tapping the spine gently with the balls of his fingers.

Suddenly White Fang's head came forward and nudged his way between the master's arm and body. Here, hidden from view, except for his ears, no longer growling, White Fang continued to nudge and snuggle. The two men looked at each other. Scott's eyes were shining.

"Gosh!" said Matt in an awestricken voice. "I always insisted that wolf was a dog. Look at him!"

With Scott's return, White Fang rapidly recovered and regained his place as leader among the other dogs.

One night, not long after Scott's return, Scott and Matt heard a noise outside the cabin. A wild scream pierced the silence. "The wolf's got someone," Matt said.

"Bring a light!" Scott shouted as he sprang outside.

Matt followed with the lamp. By its light, they saw Beauty Smith lying on his back in the snow, trying to shield

himself from White Fang's teeth.

In an instant, Scott pulled White Fang away.

"Tried to steal you, eh? And you wouldn't have it! Well, well, he made a mistake, didn't he?" Scott laughed, looking at White Fang.

"Must 'a thought he had hold of seventeen devils," Matt snickered.

White Fang, still bristling, growled and growled, the fur on his back slowly lying down, the crooning note remote and dim, but growing in his throat.

CHAPTER 18

The Voyage Home

Something was in the air. White Fang sensed it. He had seen luggage on the floor of the cabin. He knew his master was leaving again. And, just like before, White Fang knew that he was going to be left behind.

"I believe that wolf's on to you," Matt said. "He knows you're leaving."

Scott looked sadly across at his companion. "What can I do with a wolf in California?" he asked. "There's no place for him there."

"I know," Matt answered.

Scott looked at White Fang. "It would never do," he said decisively.

White Fang grew more restless. He dogged his master's heels if Scott left the

cabin, and he haunted the front porch when Scott remained inside. Then, one day, Scott called White Fang into the cabin.

"You poor boy," he said gently, rubbing White Fang's ears and tapping his spine. "I'm hitting the long trail, old man, where you cannot follow. Now give me a growl—a last, good, good-bye growl."

White Fang refused to growl. Instead, after a wistful, searching look, he snuggled in, burrowing his head between his master's arm and body.

"You've got to cut it short," Matt called when they heard the steamboat's whistle blow. "Be sure to lock the front door. I'll go out the back."

The two doors slammed in unison. Outside, Scott said, "Take good care of him, Matt. Write and let me know how he gets along."

"Sure," Matt answered as they stopped to listen. White Fang was howling as dogs howl when their masters have died.

The *Aurora* was the first steamboat of the year headed for California. The decks were jammed with prosperous adventurers and broken gold seekers, eager to get to California. Near the gangplank, Scott shook Matt's hand. When Scott looked up, he saw White Fang sitting on the deck several feet away, watching them.

Scott called White Fang. When the dog was closer, Scott could see that his underbelly was cut up.

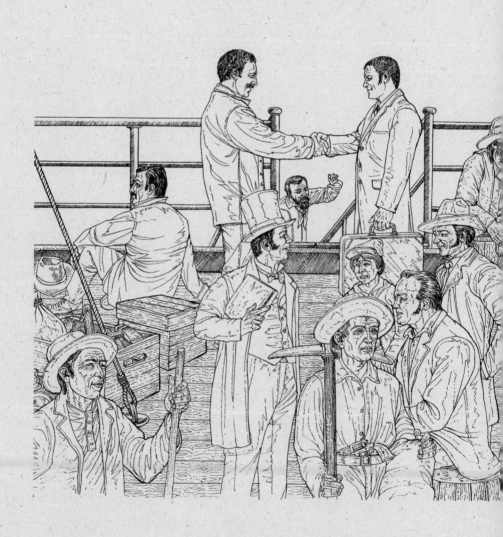

"He must have gone through the window," Matt said.

Scott was not listening. He was thinking. The *Aurora*'s whistle hooted a final boarding call. Men were scurrying down the gangplank to the shore. Matt loosened the bandana from his own neck and started to put it around White Fang's. Scott grasped Matt's hand.

"Good-bye, Matt, old man. You don't have to write. I'm taking him with me. I'll write to you about him."

Matt paused halfway down the gangplank. "He'll never stand the climate!" he shouted back. "Unless you clip him in warm weather!"

The gangplank was hauled in from the bank. Scott waved a last good-bye to his friend. Then he turned and bent over White Fang, who was standing by his side. He patted the responsive head and rubbed the flattening ears.

CHAPTER 19

The Southland

When Scott and White Fang landed in San Francisco, there were no log cabins. Instead, White Fang saw towering buildings. Now, the powers of these men seemed greater than ever.

Scott put White Fang into a baggage car and chained him in a corner in the midst of heaped trunks and valises.

White Fang thought he had been deserted, until he smelled his master's canvas bags near him. He proceeded to guard them.

"About time you came," growled the car's driver, when Scott appeared at the door. "That dog of yours won't let me lay a finger on your stuff."

When White Fang emerged from the car, he saw that the nightmare city was gone. Now he saw a beautiful country, streaming with sunshine.

A carriage was waiting for them. A couple approached Scott. White Fang became enraged when the woman put her arms around Scott's neck.

"It's all right, Mother," Scott said. He kept a tight hold on White Fang and placated him. "He thought you were going to injure me, and he wouldn't stand for it. He'll learn soon enough."

Scott's mother looked at White Fang. He snarled and glared viciously.

Scott spoke softly to White Fang until he had quieted the animal. Then Scott's voice became firm.

"Down, sir! Down with you!" Scott had taught him to do this, and White Fang obeyed, though reluctantly.

The people boarded the carriage and took off. White Fang ran swiftly to keep up with the horses and carriage that carried his master.

Soon the carriage rode through a stone gateway and between a double row of arched and interlacing walnut trees. On either side stretched lawns, their broad sweep broken here and there by great sturdy-limbed oaks. In the near distance, in contrast with the fresh green of the tended grass, sun-burned hayfields showed tan and gold.

Tawny hills and upland pastures stretched beyond the fields. At the head of the lawn, on the first soft swell from the valley level, sat a large house.

White Fang was looking at his new home when a sheepdog challenged him. It was a female. The law of his kind did not allow him to attack her.

To her, White Fang was a wolf, an animal that had preyed upon her flocks from the time sheep were first herded. No matter how White Fang tried to avoid her, she remained between him and the way he wanted to go.

"Here, Collie!" called the strange man in the carriage.

Scott laughed. "Never mind, Father. It is good discipline. White Fang will have to learn many things. It's just as well that he begins now."

The carriage drove on, and Collie still blocked White Fang's way as they ran. They raced each other forward. As he rounded the house to the porch, White Fang reached the carriage. It had stopped. Still running at top speed, White Fang was attacked from the side. It came from a deerhound.

White Fang barely missed the hound's throat. The master ran to help, but he was too far away. It was Collie that saved the hound's life. She struck White Fang at right angles in the midst of his spring, and again White Fang was knocked off his feet and rolled over.

Then the master arrived. With one hand, he held White Fang, while Scott's father called off the dogs.

"I say, this is a pretty warm reception for a poor lone wolf from the Arctic," Scott said, while White Fang calmed down under his caressing hand. "In all his life, he's only been known once to go off his feet, and here he's been put down twice in thirty seconds."

After the carriage had been driven away, more men came out of the house. Some stood nearby, while two others hugged Scott. The men approached White Fang, but he snarled. Scott told the men to stay back. White Fang leaned in close against his master's legs and received reassuring pats on the head.

Under the command, "Dick! Lie down, sir!" the hound had gone up the steps to the porch. One of the women tended Collie, who was whining and restless.

The men started up the steps to enter the house. They decided that White Fang should go inside. They did not want any more fighting.

White Fang walked stiff-legged up the steps and across the porch, with his tail rigidly erect. He kept his eyes on Dick. He was alert to whatever might be inside the house. Nothing seemed dangerous, so he rested, with a contented grunt, at his master's feet.

CHAPTER 20

A New Family

In Sierra Vista, which was the name of Scott's father's place, White Fang quickly began to make himself at home. He had learned to adapt himself to changing circumstances, from famine and Indian camps to gold rush towns and steamboats.

He had no more trouble with the dogs. They knew more about the Southland men than he did, and in their eyes, White Fang had been accepted when he was allowed inside the house.

Although Dick accepted White Fang as an addition to the household, White Fang would not befriend him. It wasn't his way, so they tolerated each other.

Collie accepted White Fang, but she did not leave him in peace. His instinct would not permit him to attack her, while her persistence would not permit him to ignore her. When she rushed at him, he turned his fur-protected shoulder to her sharp teeth and walked away stiff-legged and proud. He ignored her whenever it was possible, and tried to keep out of her way.

White Fang had much to learn about living in the Southland. First, there was the family of his master. As Mitsah and Kloo-kooch had belonged to Gray Beaver, he knew that everyone at Sierra Vista belonged to Weedon Scott.

There were Scott's parents, Judge Scott and his wife. There were Scott's two sisters, Beth and Mary. There were his wife, Alice, and then there were his children, Weedon, Jr., and Maud.

What the master valued, White Fang also valued. What was dear to the master was to be cherished by White Fang

and guarded carefully. Eventually he even came to enjoy being with the master's children.

White Fang liked to lie at Judge Scott's feet on the porch when he read the newspaper, from time to time favoring White Fang with a look or a word. But when Scott appeared, White Fang's attention centered on his master.

White Fang allowed all the members of the family to pet him, but he never gave them what he gave the master. No

caress of theirs could put the love-croon into his throat, or would persuade him into snuggling against them. This expression of absolute trust he reserved for the master alone.

Outside the household there was even more for White Fang to learn. The cuff of the master's hand and the censure of the master's voice were hard lessons. Because of White Fang's great love, a cuff from the master hurt him far more than any beating Gray Beaver or Beauty Smith had ever given him. They had hurt the flesh of him only. Beneath the flesh, the spirit had still raged, splendid and invincible. With the master, the cuff was always too light to hurt the flesh, yet it went deeper. It was an expression of the master's disapproval, and White Fang's spirit wilted under it.

Usually, the master's voice was sufficient. By Scott's voice, White Fang knew whether he did right or wrong. By it, he gauged his conduct and actions. It was the compass by which he steered and learned to chart the manners of a new land and life.

White Fang had to learn which animals he could hunt and which he had to leave alone. One day he came upon a chicken that had escaped from the chicken yard. White Fang's natural impulse was to eat it. Later in the day, he found another stray chicken near the stables. He ate that chicken, too.

"He'll learn to leave chickens alone," Scott said. "But I can't teach him the lesson until I catch him in the act."

Two nights later, Scott got his chance. White Fang raided the chicken house. He killed fifty white Leghorn hens. The master's lips tightened as he faced the disagreeable task. Then he spoke harshly and held White Fang's nose down to the hens. At the same time, he cuffed White Fang soundly. White Fang never raided a chicken-roost again.

Later, sitting with Scott and Beth at the lunch table, Judge Scott said, "You can never cure a chicken-killer."

Weedon Scott did not agree with his father. "I'll tell you what I'll do," he challenged. "I'll lock White Fang in with the chickens all afternoon."

"But think of the chickens," Judge Scott said.

"For every chicken he kills, I'll pay you one gold dollar," his son added.

"But if you win, you should penalize

Father, too," said Beth, championing White Fang. Judge Scott nodded his head in agreement.

"All right," Weedon Scott said. "And if, at the end of the afternoon, White Fang hasn't harmed a chicken, for every ten minutes of the time he has spent in the yard, you will have to say to him, just as if you were sitting on the bench and solemnly passing judgment, 'White Fang, you are smarter than I thought.'"

Later, when White Fang was placed in the chicken yard, he lay down and went to sleep. Once, he got up and walked to the trough for a drink of water. He ignored the chickens and grew bored. After almost three hours, Scott called White Fang. The dog leaped to the roof of the chicken house and then to the ground outside.

On the porch, before the delighted family, Judge Scott, face-to-face with White Fang, slowly and solemnly, repeated, "White Fang, you are smarter

than I thought."

Life for White Fang in the Santa Clara Valley seemed complicated after the simplicities of the Northland. He learned to leave the domesticated animals alone, but found that he could still hunt wild animals like jackrabbits. He was not supposed to fight, but he learned that there was an exception to that rule, too.

Whenever he went to town with the master, three dogs from the saloon always rushed upon him. Knowing his deadly method of fighting, Scott continued to reinforce to White Fang that he must not fight. White Fang snarled to keep the dogs at a distance.

Once, the men from the saloon encouraged their dogs to attack White Fang. Scott stopped the carriage and nodded his head.

"Go get them, old fellow. Eat them up," Scott said.

White Fang no longer hesitated. He turned and leaped silently among his enemies. All three faced him and were defeated. The story of White Fang's victory spread up and down the valley. From then on, men saw to it that their dogs did not threaten White Fang.

CHAPTER 21
Learning to Love

The months came and went. There was plenty of food and no work in the Southland. White Fang lived a prosperous and happy life. Human kindness was like the sun shining upon him, and he flourished like a flower planted in good soil.

He began to get along with the other dogs, but Collie remained the one trial in his life. She followed him like a policeman around the stable and the hounds. If he even glanced at a pigeon or chicken, she would bark and whine. His favorite way of ignoring her was to lie down, with his head on his forepaws, and pretend to be asleep. This always silenced her.

White Fang had never been very demonstrative. Beyond his snuggling and crooning, he had no way of expressing his love. He learned to laugh at himself. When Scott laughed at him in a good-natured way, he accepted it.

Likewise, he learned to romp with his master. At the end of such a romp, Scott's arms went around White Fang's neck and shoulders, while White Fang crooned and growled his love song. But nobody else ever romped with White

Fang. He did not permit it. He loved with a single heart.

One of White Fang's chief duties was to run alongside his master's horse when Scott went riding. The longest day never tired White Fang. His was the gait of the wolf—smooth, tireless, and effortless. At the end of fifty miles, he would come in happily ahead of the horse.

While riding with Scott, White Fang discovered another way to express his love. He barked. It was remarkable, in that he did it twice only in all his life. The first time, he had barked at the master's kicking and rearing horse as he fretted over the master's safety.

The second time White Fang barked, Scott was not even there. A jackrabbit had jumped in front of the horse suddenly and the horse reared up, spilling Scott to the ground. The fall broke the master's leg.

"Go on home and tell them what's happened to me. Home with you, you

wolf. Get along home!" Scott said.

White Fang did not want to leave his master, but he did as he was commanded. He knew the meaning of the word "home." He ran to the porch, where the family was sitting.

"Weedon's back," Weedon's mother announced.

White Fang was very agitated. The family did not know why. Growling savagely, White Fang sprang up, upsetting the children. Weedon's mother called

them to her and comforted them, telling them not to bother White Fang.

"A wolf is a wolf!" Judge Scott commented. "There is no trusting one."

"But he is not all wolf," Beth said.

White Fang continued to growl. He turned to Scott's wife. She screamed as he seized her dress in his teeth and pulled on it until the frail fabric tore.

By this time, White Fang had caught their attention. Beth knew that something must be wrong. He had stopped growling and was standing, head up, looking into their faces.

"I hope he is not going mad," said Weedon's mother. "I told Weedon that I was afraid the warm climate would not agree with an Arctic animal."

"He's trying to speak to us," Beth announced. And suddenly, for the second and last time in his life, White Fang barked.

"Something has happened to Weedon," his wife said decisively.

By now, they were all on their feet. White Fang ran down the steps, looking back for them to follow. He had barked and was understood.

After this, he found a warmer place in the hearts of the Sierra Vista people.

The days went by swiftly. During White Fang's second winter in the Southland, he made a strange discovery: Collie's teeth were no longer sharp. There was a playfulness about her nips and a gentleness that prevented them from hurting him. He forgot that she had made life a burden to him.

One day, she led him off on a long chase through the back-pasture land into the woods. It was the afternoon that his master was to ride, and White Fang knew it. The horse stood saddled and waiting at the door. White Fang hesitated, but something led him on. It was deeper than all of the laws he had learned from men, than the customs that had molded him, than his love for

his master, than the very will to live.

Collie nipped him and scampered off. He turned and followed after. The master rode alone that day; and in the woods, side by side, White Fang ran with Collie, as his mother, Kiche, and old One Eye had run many years before in the silent Northland forest.

CHAPTER 22

The Blessed Wolf

At this time, the newspapers were full of the daring escape of a convict, Jim Hall, from San Quentin Prison. He was a ferocious man who had a grudge against Judge Scott. The judge had passed a sentence upon him, sending him to jail for fifty years.

Jim Hall hated all things. He was armed and dangerous. A substantial reward had been offered for his capture. People organized a manhunt to find him, eager to earn the reward.

The bloodhounds vainly searched. In the meantime, the family at Sierra Vista read newspapers not so much with interest as with anxiety. The women were afraid. Judge Scott tried to allay their fears. He laughed, telling them not to worry, but they remained alarmed.

Of course White Fang did not understand their fear. But between White Fang and Alice, the master's wife, there existed a secret. Each night, after everyone was sound asleep, she rose and let in White Fang to sleep in the big hall. White Fang was not a housedog, and he was not permitted to sleep in the house. So early each morning, she slipped down-

stairs and let him out before the family was awake.

Then one night, while everyone in the house slept, White Fang heard a noise. A stranger was in the house. The strange man walked softly, but White Fang walked more softly. White Fang had no clothes to rub against the flesh of his body. He knew the advantage of surprise.

The stranger paused at the foot of the staircase and listened. The staircase led to his master and his master's dearest possessions. White Fang bristled, but waited. The stranger's foot lifted. He was beginning the ascent.

All at once, White Fang struck. He lifted his body into the air and landed on the stranger's back. White Fang clung with his forepaws to the man's shoulders, at the same time burying his fangs into the back of the man's neck. He clung for a moment, long enough to drag the man over backward. Together, they crashed to the

floor. White Fang leaped clear and, as the man struggled to rise, came in again with slashing fangs.

Sierra Vista awoke in alarm. The noise from downstairs sounded like a mass of battling fiends. There were revolver shots. A man screamed. There was loud snarling and growling, and over all arose the sounds of furniture tumbling and glass crashing.

Almost as quickly as it had arisen, the commotion died away. The struggle had not lasted more than three minutes. The frightened household gathered at the top of the stairway. Weedon Scott pressed a button, and light flooded the staircase and the downstairs hall. Then he and Judge Scott, revolvers in hand, cautiously descended.

There was no need for this caution. White Fang had done his work. In the midst of the wreckage, partly on his side, his face hidden by an arm, lay Jim Hall. Weedon Scott bent over him, pushed away the arm, and turned the man's face upward. A gaping throat explained what had happened.

The men turned to White Fang. He, too, was lying on his side. His eyes were closed, but the lids lifted slightly in an effort to look at them. He tried to wag his tail. Weedon Scott patted him. His throat rumbled a weak growl. His eyelids drooped and went shut. White Fang's whole body seemed to have collapsed and flattened out upon the floor.

"He's done in, poor devil," Weedon Scott said sighing.

"We'll see about that," Judge Scott said as he started for the telephone.

Soon a surgeon arrived. Dawn was breaking through the windows and overpowering the electric lights. With the exception of the children, the whole family gathered around the surgeon to hear his verdict.

"Frankly, he has one chance in a thousand to survive," the surgeon

announced after he had worked for more than an hour on White Fang.

"One broken hind leg," he went on. "Three broken ribs, one punctured lung. He's been shot and has internal injuries. One chance in a thousand is optimistic. He hasn't one chance in ten thousand."

"But he mustn't lose any chance that might be of help to him," Judge Scott exclaimed. "Never mind expense. Do whatever can be done to save him."

"Of course, I understand," said the surgeon. "He must be nursed as you would nurse a sick human being or a sick child."

White Fang received good care. The girls, who undertook the task, rejected Judge Scott's suggestion of a trained nurse. They tended him well. White Fang won out on the one chance in ten thousand denied him by the surgeon.

White Fang had come from the Wild, where the weak perish early. His endurance was part of his inheritance from his mother and father. Fiercely, he clung to life.

White Fang lingered on through the weeks in his bandages and casts. He slept for hours and dreamed a lot. All of the ghosts of his past visited him. Kiche, Gray Beaver, Lip-lip, and the cries of the puppy pack came to him in his dreams. He relived his days with Beauty Smith and the fights he had fought. At such times, he whimpered and snarled in his sleep.

Finally the last bandage and the last plaster cast were taken off. All of Sierra Vista gathered around. The master rubbed White Fang's ears. The master's wife called him the "Blessed Wolf," a name that was taken up by all of White Fang's admirers.

He tried to rise. After several attempts, he fell down from weakness. All of the strength had gone out of his limbs. He felt ashamed of his weakness, as though

he were failing his master. Because of this, he made heroic efforts to rise. At last, he stood on his four legs, tottering and swaying back and forth.

"The Blessed Wolf!" the women cried in unison.

Judge Scott surveyed them triumphantly. "Just as I contended all along. No mere dog could have done what he did. He's a wolf," he said.

"A Blessed Wolf," Judge Scott's wife corrected.

"Yes, a Blessed Wolf," Judge Scott agreed. "And, henceforth, that will be my name for him."

"He'll have to learn to walk again," the surgeon said. "He might as well start now. Take him outside."

He went out like a king, with all of Sierra Vista around him. He was very weak, and when he reached the lawn, he lay down and rested for a while.

Then, little spurts of strength began to return to White Fang's muscles. He reached the stables and there, in the doorway, lay Collie. Six pudgy puppies played around her in the sun.

White Fang looked on with a wondering eye. Collie snarled a warning. He was careful to keep his distance. Gently, the master pushed one puppy toward White Fang. He bristled suspiciously, but the master's reassuring glance let him know that all was well. Collie, clasped in the arms of one of the women, jealously watched White Fang.

The puppy crawled in front of him. White Fang cocked his ears and watched it curiously. Then their noses touched, and he felt the warm little tongue of the puppy on his snout. White Fang's tongue went out. He licked the puppy's face.

Handclapping and smiles from the Scotts greeted the performance. White Fang was surprised. He looked at them in a puzzled way.

Then he lay down, his ears cocked, his head on one side, as he watched the puppy. The other puppies crawled toward him, to Collie's great disgust. White Fang let his puppies frolic and tumble over him.

At first, amid the applause, White Fang betrayed some of his old awkwardness. This passed away as the puppies' antics continued, and he lay with half-shut, patient eyes in the sun. All of his loved ones surrounded White Fang. Truly, he had found a home.

About the Author

John (Jack) London was born in 1876 in San Francisco, California. He spent most of his childhood in the Bay Area of California before settling in Oakland.

London completed grade school, but at the age of fourteen he went to work to support his family. He served on a fish patrol and hunted seals in the the Pacific Ocean, among other pursuits. After he got into trouble with the law, he went back to school. He was accepted into college, but stayed for only six months.

London then traveled to seek his fortune in Canada's Yukon Territory during the gold rush. When he returned to San Francisco, he began writing about his adventures. In addition to short stories, newspaper articles, and essays, London wrote a number of classics, including *White Fang* and *The Call of the Wild*.

He died in 1916 in Santa Rosa, California.

Treasury of Illustrated Classics